**Once upon a time in a little village called Zambo, deep in the African jungle, there lived a little boy called Ariyo who lived with his Mummy and Daddy.**

**One day, Ariyo was playing in the garden. It was hot and windy! It hadn't rained in Zambo village for many months.**

**Suddenly he heard his Daddy call his name."Ariyo! We are very thirsty and hot and there is no water at home. Can you go down to the well near the river and fetch some water please?"**

Ariyo picked up his bucket and headed down to the river.

On his way to the river, he was enjoying the sound of crickets, when suddenly, his friend Akima the monkey came to him and said, "I am very thirsty and hot Ariyo, can you get me some water?". Ariyo responded and said "don't worry Akima, I will get you some water on my way back".

Ariyo continued to whistle as he walked down to the river. Not long after he bumped into Maisy the yellow snake. She slithered towards him and said "I am very thirsty and hot Ariyo, can you get me some water please?". Ariyo responded and said "don't worry Maisy, I will get you some water on my way back".

Ariyo continued to walk to the river, when he saw Archie the camel panting for water. He said "I have been to the desert and I am very thirsty and hot Ariyo, can you get me some water please?". Ariyo responded and said "don’t worry Archie, I will get you some water on my way back".

Just before he got to the well, he saw Darko the Rhinoceros, who charged at him to beg for water. Ariyo responded and said "don’t worry Darko, I will get you some water on my way back".

Ariyo got to the river and filled his bucket with fresh water. He was very happy.

On his way back he stopped by Darko the Rhinoceros, who had a big glug of the water. Darko said, "can I have some more?" Ariyo said, "sorry, others need to drink too. You need to say thank you before asking for more". Darko said "thank you for the water" and he left.

Not long after, he saw Archie the Camel still panting so he gave him some water. Archie said,"thank you for the water". Ariyo replied, "you are welcome" and left.

He continued his journey home and met Maisy the snake coming out of her log pile house. He offered her some water and she was very grateful.

Finally, just before Ariyo got home, Akima jumped down from the tree and said "Hey Ariyo, do you still have some water for me?". Ariyo said "of course, there you go" and he offered Akima some water.

Then Ariyo looked into his bucket and realized it was empty. All his friends had finished his water. He was very sad as it was too late and dark to go back to the river.

**Ariyo started to cry and began to sing as he made his way back home.**

**Suddenly, the thunderstorm sounded loudly, the cloud darkened, and it started to rain.**

**The rain poured down pitter patter, pitter patter and as soon as Ariyo's bucket was filled to the brim, the rain stopped.**

Ariyo was so amazed. As soon as he got home, he gave his Mummy and Daddy some water.

Ariyo's daddy had a drink of the water and he said "hmm this is very fresh!".

He said "thank you to Ariyo. You did very well today”. Ariyo was very happy.

That night he went to bed and thanked the Zambo Gods for the miracle. Suddenly he was very tired. It had been a long day. He lay his head on his pillow and fell fast asleep.

# MORALS

1.Sharing is caring – Always share with others
2. Remember to say thank you when people offer you something
3. Always be happy to help your mummy and daddy
4. Remember to say please when asking for something
5. Sometimes miracles happen when we help others.We may just get a surprising reward
6. Remember to drink lots of water to keep you healthy and hydrated always.

Printed in Great Britain
by Amazon

10792902R00027